Best of all everyone liked to hear Turtle sing.

She liked to sing with her best friend Little Bear.

Everyone said Turtle had a **beautiful voice**.

But Turtle was shy. She was often **too shy** to answer Miss Bird's questions in class.

She was often too shy to say 'hello' to visitors.
And when Turtle felt shy she **hid in her shell**.

One day Miss Bird had some **exciting news**. She said that Jungle School was going to hold a talent show. She said that all the families were to be invited. She said everyone had to think of something exciting to do in the show.

Rhino and Giraffe said they wanted do magic
tricks. Miss Bird said that was a **good idea**.
Elephant and Lion wanted to play the drums.
Miss Bird said that was a good idea, too.

Monkey and Hippo said they wanted to do
a dance. They said they were really good at
dancing. Miss Bird wrote down everyone's ideas.

At playtime, Little Bear asked Turtle if she would like to sing a song with her at the talent show. She said it would be **fun**. Turtle said she would be too shy to sing on a stage in front of lots of people. She said it might be **scary**.

But Turtle couldn't stop thinking about the show. She loved singing with Little Bear, but she felt **too shy**. Turtle was sad. She went to see Miss Bird.

Miss Bird said everyone felt shy sometimes. She said when she was a little bird, she was so shy at birthday parties that she **hid her head** under her wing. Turtle was very surprised. She couldn't imagine Miss Bird **ever** feeling shy.

Miss Bird told her that when she felt shy she always took a **deep breath**. She said it made her feel better. Turtle took a deep breath. She felt **much better**.

Miss Bird said that when Turtle felt shy she could **talk to her friends**. She said this would make her feel better. Turtle said she could talk to Little Bear. Miss Bird said Little Bear would be a **good friend** to talk to.

Then Miss Bird asked Turtle how she could **help herself** to sing on stage with Little Bear. Turtle had a good think. She said she would feel much better if she sang inside her shell. Miss Bird said that was **a very good idea**.

At last it was the night of the talent show. All the mums and dads, grannies and grandpas were there. Turtle started to feel shy. She began to worry. Then she remembered what Miss Bird told her. She took a **deep breath**.
She felt **a bit better**.

Then she told Little Bear she felt shy. Little Bear told her **not to worry**. She said she would be right beside her **all the time**.

Soon it was time for Turtle and Little Bear
to sing their song.

Turtle hid in her shell, but she **sang beautifully**.
It was the best she had ever sung.

When they had finished singing, **everyone clapped… and cheered**! Turtle was so surprised she popped her head out of her shell to look. Everyone was clapping and cheering as loud as they could. Turtle enjoyed it so much she gave a **little bow**.

After the show Miss Bird said everyone had **done well**. She said Turtle had done **really well**.

Turtle said she was glad she sang with Little Bear.
Best of all she was **glad** she came out of her shell
because it was lovely to see everyone clapping
and cheering.

# A note about sharing this book

The *Behaviour Matters* series has been developed to provide
a starting point for further discussion on children's
behaviour both in relation to themselves and others.
The series is set in the jungle with animal
characters reflecting typical behaviour
traits often seen in young children.

**Turtle Comes Out of her Shell**
This story looks at why some people feel
uncomfortable in certain situations and
how they can overcome their shyness to
join in with others.

**How to use the book**
The book is designed for adults to share with either an individual child,
or a group of children, and as a starting point for discussion.

The book also provides visual support and repeated words and phrases
to build reading confidence.

**Before reading the story**
Choose a time to read when you and the children are relaxed and have
time to share the story.

Spend time looking at the illustrations and talk about what the book
might be about before reading it together.

Encourage children to employ a phonics first approach to tackling
new words by sounding the words out.

**After reading, talk about the book with the children:**

- Talk about the story with the children. Encourage them to retell the events in chronological order.

- Talk about Turtle's shyness. When does she feel shy in the story? Ask the children if they have ever felt shy. What were the circumstances? Examples may be starting a new school, or getting to know new neighbours etc. Invite the children to share their experiences.

- Spend time talking about events that happen in school for example, school plays, concerts or even having to answer questions in class. Which situations make the children feel anxious? Point out that almost everyone gets butterflies in their tummies when they have to perform on stage – even famous actors!

- Discuss ways of overcoming anxiety and shyness. What did Miss Bird suggest to Turtle to help her? As a class invite the children all to stand and to take a slow breath in and out. How did it make them feel?

- Ask the children if they know of other ways of making themselves feel calm. They may like to have a favourite toy with them when they feel anxious. They may seek out a friend to help them.

- Place the children into groups. Ask them to brainstorm how they would help a friend overcome shyness and anxiety to perform in a school production. They may for example suggest that the shy person could stand by their best friend, or choose not to stand in the front line.

- At the end of the session, invite each group to share their findings with the others. Together, draw up a list of useful strategies that would help a shy person in such situations.

For Isabelle, William A, William G, George, Max, Emily, Leo, Caspar, Felix, Tabitha, Phoebe and Harry – S.G.

First published in Great Britain in 2018
by The Watts Publishing Group

Text © The Watts Publishing Group 2018
Illustrations © Trevor Dunton 2018

The right of Trevor Dunton to be identified as the illustrator
of this Work has been asserted in accordance with the
Copyright, Designs and Patents Act, 1988.
All rights reserved.

Series Editor: Jackie Hamley
Series Designer: Cathryn Gilbert

A CIP catalogue record for this book is
available from the British Library.

ISBN 978 1 4451 5853 2 (HB)
ISBN 978 1 4451 5854 9 (PB)

Printed in China

Franklin Watts
An imprint of
Hachette Children's Group
Part of The Watts Publishing Group
Carmelite House
50 Victoria Embankment
London EC4Y 0DZ

An Hachette UK Company
www.hachette.co.uk

www.franklinwatts.co.uk

FSC
www.fsc.org
MIX
Paper from
responsible sources
FSC® C104740